For Mom

Copyright © 2018 by Carin Bramsen
All rights reserved. Published in the United States by Random House Children's Books,
a division of Penguin Random House LLC, New York.
Random House and the colophon are registered trademarks of Penguin Random House LLC.
Visit us on the Web! randomhousekids.com
Educators and librarians, for a variety of teaching tools, visit us at RHTeachersLibrarians.com
Library of Congress Cataloging-in-Publication Data
Names: Bramsen, Carin, author.
Title: Sleepover Duck! / by Carin Bramsen.
Description: First edition. | New York : Random House Children's Books [2018]
Summary: Duck and Cat have their very first sleepover in the barn.
Identifiers: LCCN 2016046616 (print) | LCCN 2017021107 (ebook)
ISBN 978-0-385-38417-9 (hc) | ISBN 978-0-375-97345-1 (glb) | ISBN 978-0-385-38418-6 (ebook)
Subjects: | CYAC: Stories in rhyme. | Sleepovers—Fiction. | Ducks—Fiction. | Cats—Fiction. |
Friendship—Fiction. | Domestic animals—Fiction.
Classification: LCC PZ8.3.B7324 (ebook) | LCC PZ8.3.B7324 Sl 2017 (print) | DDC [E]—dc23
MANUFACTURED IN CHINA
10 9 8 7 6 5 4 3 2 1   First Edition
Book design by Tracy Tyler

epover Duck!

Carin Bramsen

Random House 🏠 New York

Hey, Cat! My mom said it's all right to sleep inside the barn tonight.

A slumber party here with me?

We'll have a slumber
JAMBOREEEEE!

It's nice and quiet
here in back.

A *sleepover.*
I'm all a-quack.

Yippeeee!

**We finally get a chance
to do the slumber party dance!**

Now let the slumber games begin. . . .

Whoever sleeps is OUT!

Zzzzzzz . . .

You win.

HEY, CAT!

Must we nod off right now?
Alas, I've just forgotten how.

Well, lie down first. Try breathing deep.
It's not so hard to fall asleep.

Then I'll lie here, if you don't mind.
Oh, thanks. That's better. You're too kind.
My friend, this party is a ball.

Woo-hoooo!

Was that a party call?

Hey, Cat! Let's see if that woo-hoo means someone wants to party, too.

Okay, but let's not wake the house. . . .

I'll be as quiet as a mouse.

Excuse me, did you say **woo-hoo?**

No, dear. I normally say **moooo.**

Hello! Was that *your* party cry?

No, I just whispered, "Hush-a-bye."

Did you call out woo-hoo, Ms. Sheep?

No, hon. I'm counting down to sleep.

Ms. Sow's asleep.
Her piglets, too.

So where's the one
who said **woo-hoo**?

I think that we've looked everywhere.

Let's search the hayloft, way up there!

Duck, have you found
who said **woo-hoo**?

Aha. I see it's time to rest.
Sweet dreams to you, my duckie guest.

Yooo-hooooo!

Why did you close your eyes?
I thought this was a party, guys.

Why, *that's* the voice that said **woo-hoo!**
The secret party guest is *you!*

How do you dooooo? Owlette's my name,
and hide-and-seek's my favorite game.

This party night
has been the best!

But maybe now
you'd like to rest.

My friends, till next time.
Toodle-ooooo!

Good night, Owlette.
Great meeting you!

You do seem kind of sleepy, Cat.
But I just say **woo-hoo** to that!

There's nothing I would rather do
than get all tuckered out with you.